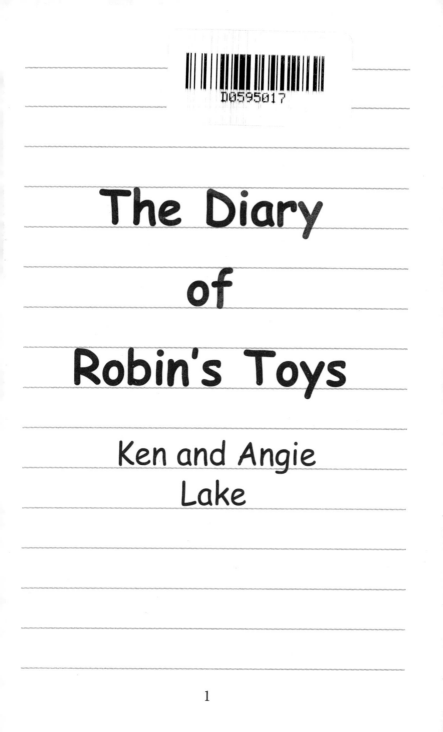

The Diary of Robin's Toys

Ken and Angie Lake

Bertie

the Bee

Published by Sweet Cherry Publishing Limited
53 St. Stephens Road,
Leicester, LE2 1GH
United Kingdom
First Published in the UK in 2013

ISBN: 978-1-78226-021-9
Text: © Ken and Angie Lake 2013
Illustrations: (c) Vishnu Madhav and Joyson Loitongbam,
Creative Books

Title: Bertie the Bee - The Diaries of Robin's Toys

Printed and Bound By Nutech Print Services, India

Every Toy Has a Story to Tell

Have you ever seen an old toy, perhaps in a cupboard, or in the attic or loft? Have you ever seen how sad they look at car boot sales, unwanted and unloved? Well, look at them closely, because every toy has a story to tell, and the older, the more decrepit, the more scruffy, the more tatty the toy is, the more interesting its story could be. Here are just a few of those toys and their stories.

10th June, 09.25

Sunday was Robin's favourite day; he looked forward to it all week. It was the day his grandad picked him up in his little red car and took him to the car boot sale.

If he had been good during the week and helped his mum, then Grandad would give him 50 pence to spend on a toy of his choice.

But it was always more exciting than that. You see, Grandad had special powers. He could cast a secret spell and make the toys talk. Some of the stories they would tell ... well, you just wouldn't believe them!

Robin really hoped that this week he'd find some kind of football-related toy. Robin played in the local football league and the team met every Saturday morning to practise. This year so far they'd done very well and were one of the top teams in their age group. And a lot of that was thanks to one little boy called Bruce.

Bruce was the son of the team coach, and he was so eager to impress his dad that he always turned up super early to help get everything ready before the rest of the team arrived.

Coach Dickinson took his football coaching very seriously ... perhaps a bit too much for a man of his size. They had often seen him puffing and panting as he raced towards the ice cream van.

Coach Dickinson was very proud of his son Bruce and his commitment to the team. When there was work to be done, like flyers to be made, equipment to be cleaned or kit to be ordered, Bruce always put his hand up and shouted enthusiastically, "I'll do it!"

The problem was, that everyone else enjoyed doing things too, but because they didn't get to join in making the flyers or helping out, it was a bit boring for them.

Last weekend, Bruce had been really upset. As usual he had volunteered to tidy up and clean all the equipment. And to make flyers to let all the parents know where the next match would be held. And then to phone the uniform suppliers to order new uniforms.

Unfortunately, the football equipment he was supposed to put away had gone missing. Then the flyers he made had the wrong date and time on them. And the final problem was that when the uniforms arrived, they were all the wrong colour! They were supposed to be black with red stripes, but were black with yellow stripes!

It seemed obvious to Robin that although Bruce Dickinson was a real trooper and only wanted to help, he had definitely taken on far too much work.

It was a warm and sunny Sunday morning and Robin was staring out of the window, waiting for Grandad to arrive. He noticed a bee buzzing from flower to flower, doing a little dance and then buzzing on to the next one.

His mind drifted while he was waiting. The bee got him thinking about aeroplanes and things with wings. He loved anything that flew, as most boys his age did.

He wondered how many years it had been since the first man was able to fly. He had heard a story about a Greek man called Icarus who made some wings and then started to fly.

Apparently, he flew too close to the sun and the glue on his wings melted, so he came crashing down to Earth. Then Robin remembered a little rhyme from school.

There was a man called
Icarus, His wings were made of
liquorice, He flew around,
Crashed to the ground,
And then he felt ridiculous.

Actually, Robin didn't believe this story; it wasn't possible for anyone to fly just by flapping their wings. Perhaps he shouldn't look for a football-related toy; maybe something with wings would be more fun!

Beep, beep, beep, beep! It was Grandad's little red car.

"Come on, Robin, stop daydreaming. It's time to go to the car boot sale."

21

It was one of those nice summer days, you know the sort; the flowers were opening up, the leaves on the trees fresh and green. There was a wonderful scent of roses drifting on the gentle breeze, and people were smiling and laughing.

The car boot sale was crowded. There were ladies in flowery tops, men in shorts showing off their skinny white legs and children in buggies with ice cream faces.

"Where shall we look today, Robin?" Grandad asked.

"I know, let's have a look on that stall next to Nelly Knitwear. We don't often go to that one."

"Oh yes, I know, that's Jerry the Junk's stall. He does a lot of house clearances. Let's go and see what he has this week."

Jerry the Junk was a tall, cheerful man, and he was very strong, as he spent a lot of time moving heavy furniture.

He would often buy the entire contents of a house without knowing what was in it, so he'd end up with boxes of people's old clothes, papers and photographs.

This was why Jerry seemed to know a lot about other people in town. Robin had heard him say, "You should see some of the treasures I picked up last week."

And that was one of the reasons he reminded Robin of a

pirate, despite his really thick
Scottish accent.

This week, Jerry the Junk
had several boxes of baby
clothes and some computer
games. He also had lots of
books and some old records,
but Robin couldn't see any toys.

"Oh, that's disappointing, Grandad. I had a feeling he might have an unusual toy, you know, something that we don't often see; something with an interesting story to tell."

"Well, if you had that feeling, Robin, why don't you ask him?"

"Err, excuse me, Mr Junk, do you have any toys this week?"

"Ah yes, toys. I must have some real treasures, I just haven't unpacked them yet. Hang on, let me check my treasure chest in the back of the van."

So that's what he did.

Robin sorted through the cuddly toys and the dolls, but he wasn't interested in those.

"No, sorry, Mr Junk, I was really looking for something to do with football, or something that flies."

"Oh right, something that flies you say?"

Jerry the Junk reached into his van and held up a very unusual toy.

"This toy, young man, flies and does a lot more besides that."

He held out his hand and Robin looked at a big toy bee.

It had black and yellow stripes, huge eyes and a fat body. Its wings were made of loops of wire and it had a big smile on its little face.

"I was thinking more of an aeroplane, or perhaps a helicopter."

"Have you ever seen an aeroplane or a helicopter that can make honey?"

Robin had to admit that he hadn't; in fact, he had never even thought about that. So that and the bee's smile convinced him that this toy would have a good story to tell.

"It looks very interesting, but how much do you want for it?"

"Oh, give me a pound and it's yours."

"I am sorry, Mr Junk, but I only have 50 pence."

Robin looked sad; then he turned and started to walk away.

"Alright, son, come back. It's my birthday today and I am feeling generous. Here, you can have Bertie the Bee for 50p. Oh, that rhymes! I must be a poet, and I didn't know it. Oh, that rhymes as well! Shall I put him in a bag for you?"

Robin and Grandad had a final walk around the car boot sale. Grandad bought Grandma a present like he did every Sunday. He remembered she had been complaining all week about how the handle kept falling off her old frying pan.

"Harry," she would say in her angry voice, "I've had this frying pan since we were married and it keeps falling to bits. I think it's time you did something about it!"

When Grandad and Robin arrived at Grandad's house, Grandma had made some delicious iced butterfly buns for them to have with their tea.

Grandad gave Grandma her present.

"What's this?" she asked, looking puzzled.

"Well," said Grandad, "I know how attached you are to your frying pan, seeing as you've had it for such a long time, so I've bought you a new handle for it."

Grandma was confused and looked like she was about to start an argument, but she just let out a loud sigh and disappeared into the front room to get on with her knitting.

When Grandma had left, Grandad and Robin took Bertie the Bee out of the bag and put him on the kitchen table. Then Grandad cast his little spell.

"Little toy, hear this rhyme,
Let it take you back in time,
Tales of sadness or of glory,
Little toy, reveal your story."

Bertie rubbed his large eyes with his hairy legs, twitched his rear and flapped all four of his wings. He shuffled his legs

and did a little dance. Then he
stared at Robin and Grandad.

*"Hello," he said. "Who are you
two? Are you both gardeners?"*

"No, not really. My name is Robin, and this is my grandad."

"Oh, I have seen someone like Grandad before. I can't quite remember where, but it will come to me. Where is my hive and the rest of my colony?"

"Sorry, Mr Bee, we don't really know. We have just bought you from the car boot sale. We think you may have an interesting story to tell."

"You are right, I do, but do you know anything at all about bees?"

"No, not much, except that you are very busy and somehow make honey."

"Well, Robin, you are right about that. If you are both sitting comfortably, I shall tell you my story.

"Bees are insects, but don't judge us because of that. Most of us are really nice guys, and *you would not believe how useful we are.*

"There are literally thousands of different types of bees in the world, but I am a honey bee. Yes, I know that I have a sting, but I won't use it if you are nice to me.

"If I did have to use it I would die. But let's not think about that. Now, bees don't just come in boy and girl types; we have three different sorts.

"First there are Workers. That's what I am, and guess what I do? Yes, you've got it,

I work. My main job is to fly from flower to flower. Then I crawl inside and use my long tongue to get some sweet nectar, but I also collect pollen on my legs.

"Now, here is the big deal. When we are crawling around in the flowers we spread pollen from one flower to another and this pollinates them, so that they can produce seeds and fruit.

"So without the bees doing their job, there wouldn't be much food in the world. Now you can see just how important we are.

"The next sort of bees are called Drones, but not because they drone on and on and bore the other bees ... No, there must be another reason why they are called Drones, but I can't remember. It will come to me.

"These bees have a great job; they just look after the Queen Bee and make sure that she can lay lots and lots of eggs.

"There is usually only one Queen Bee in the hive. She is bigger than the others, and no, she doesn't wear a little gold crown. Her job is to lay eggs, which will hatch into new bees. You see, that's how it all works.

"It's one big team and we all work together. We live in the same big house called a hive. I'm not sure why it's called that, it just is.

"We can only work when the weather is nice. That's why we make honey, so we have food to keep us alive during the winter. It's lucky that we make enough to share it with people.

"Alright, that's a bit about bees in general, now for my story.

"When I was very young I liked to buzz around and keep the hive tidy. Well, somebody had to. With all those bees coming and going all day long, the hive would soon have been a mess if I hadn't. Yes, I was a very busy bee.

"I remember my first day at work as if it was yesterday. It was a beautiful sunny morning. It was going to be my first solo flight and I was a bit nervous. I had learned the basic skills in bee school, but the first day can always be difficult.

"I wandered down the corridor to the hive entrance and past the guards. This was an exclusive hive, so it was always guarded to keep out the riff-raff of the insect world.

"It was a big drop, so I hesitated when I got to the edge. Then one of the guards gave me a gentle smack on my bum, and that launched me into the big wide world.

"Suddenly, I was flying; I was what you might call a Free-Bee. I felt tempted to fly off and do my own thing, but fortunately, I had been trained well.

"My route had been planned for me: Fly down the lane until you get to the big oak tree, take a right and follow the path as far as the green garden shed. Stop there for a couple of minutes to get your bearings and then check out every flower in the garden.

"Although I had followed these instructions to the letter, I couldn't help thinking that it was not a very direct route; not what you could call a Bee-Line. But there were lots of bees, and I presumed that Bee Flight Control didn't want any collisions.

"I sat on the roof of the shed and looked around. Wow, this is amazing, I thought. So many different flowers. It was a mixed garden, with both vegetables, and flowers. I had been told that people eat vegetables, but only look at flowers. Strange creatures these people! So I made straight for the flower garden.

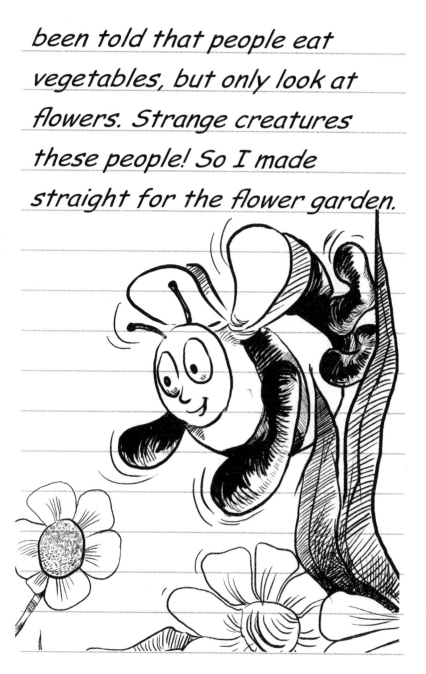

"What a fantastic mixture of colours! Bright reds, yellows, pinks, blues and lots of others which I couldn't remember the names of."

"Okay, Bertie, so what happened next?" Robin asked.

"Well, I can tell you both that I was in bee heaven. As I buzzed past the tallest and prettiest flowers, I suddenly remembered that they were called foxgloves. I couldn't quite remember why, but I knew it would come to me.

"I dived straight in to get the nectar. Wow, what scents, what colours! Then I started to gather the bright yellow pollen and stuffed it into my pollen sacks.

"These sacks are conveniently fixed to my knees. It was so much fun; you could say it was the Bees-Knees!

"I crawled into the next flower, then the next, then the next... I'd collected so much pollen that I was sure I'd bring back the most and the Queen would be very proud of me.

"It was getting late and, even though it wasn't on my route, I headed for the vegetable plot. I wasn't supposed to go there; other bees would cover that area. But I knew there was lots more pollen to collect, and I wanted to bring back the most!

"As I flew around, I realised that I knew most of the vegetables by name. There were runner beans with their red flowers, peas and broad beans with their white flowers.

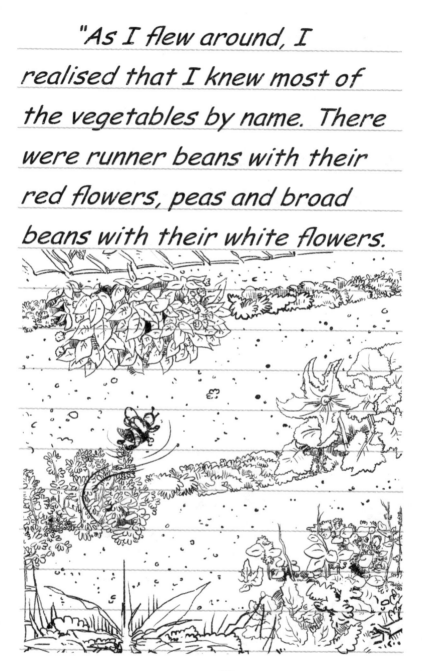

"There were lots of strawberries, raspberries and blackcurrants too and one special plant with huge yellow flowers. I had been told the name, but spelt it wrong in my final flower recognition test. It was called a courgette. I flew straight into its huge yellow flower.

"I was so busy that I hadn't noticed the time. Now, bees don't have watches - that would be silly - but I had been taught that when my pollen sacks were full it was time to go home.

"I was also full of nectar, which is very precious for the bee colony; we put it into the cells and then cover these with beeswax until it turns into honey.

"It was very late and I had to get back immediately, but I had worked so hard in the hot sun that I really needed a drink. There was a pretty pond in the corner of the garden, so I decided to have a quick drink before setting off back to the hive.

"I tried to land on a big stone in the middle, but as I landed, I slipped and went sliding down into the water. I hadn't been told about wet stones being slippery. I had just been told to avoid ponds altogether. Now I knew why!

"I buzzed and flapped as hard as I could, but I just couldn't get out of the water. The harder I tried, the worse it got. I was getting tired and started to panic. How was I going to get all this precious pollen back to the hive to help feed the new bee grubs?

"Suddenly, a strange thing
happened. A giant net scooped
me up and out of the water.
At the end of the net was a
friendly, smiling face. It was
the gardener. What a lucky
bee I was.

" 'Come on, little bee, you're not supposed to be in there,' he said. 'Now off you go back home.'

"I didn't need telling twice. Thankfully this old man knew just how important bees are, not just for his garden, but for the whole world.

"When I got back to the hive there was a real buzz in the atmosphere. Beryl Bee came up to me and said that they had all been really worried about me and were about to send out a search party. I explained what had happened and how I wanted to bring back the most pollen, but how it had all gone wrong.

"Beryl said that it's important to do your job well, but that a bee hive is a team: everybody shares the work equally.

'Look, Bertie,' she said, 'if we all did what you have done today, lots of bees would go missing all the time and their pollen would never get back to the hive. That's why we share the work equally, so hopefully, no one gets hurt.'

"I thought about what she said and realised how sharing the work is all part of being in a team."

"Oh, thank you, Bertie, that was a fascinating story! We had no idea about your society. It's so different from ours. You all work as a big team, and as we say, there is no 'I' in team. We had no idea just how important bees are to all of us."

After hearing Bertie's story, Robin had an idea. When Grandad dropped him and Bertie off at home on Sunday afternoon, Robin phoned all of his teammates and they hatched a plan to help Bruce.

On the following Saturday morning, Bruce arrived early as always, but this time he got quite a surprise. The rest of the team had arrived even earlier!

Some of the team members had gone looking for the missing equipment and had found it in the washroom. Obviously Bruce had intended to clean the equipment, but he had got distracted with something else and forgotten where he had left it. The boys had cleaned it all up and got everything ready for practice.

The rest of the team had been busy making all the flyers for the next match, with the correct date and time. Coach Dickinson made a surprise announcement.

"Thanks to all your great work, we are completely ready for practice today and for the match next week.

"I would also like to thank Bruce for ordering the black and yellow uniforms, and Robin for bringing our new team mascot, Bertie the Bee. I shall change our team name to The Busy Bees."

Everybody cheered, and Bruce understood the true meaning of teamwork.

"Now," said Coach Dickinson, "I think this calls for a celebration."

And as he ran puffing and panting behind a passing ice cream van, the boys all sat down with Bertie, the new team mascot, to listen to his story.